*Face-Off*

# *Face-Off*

by Matt Christopher

*illustrated by Harvey Kidder*

Little, Brown and Company
BOSTON    NEW YORK    TORONTO    LONDON

First Paperback Edition

Library of Congress Catalog Card No. 78-189258

ISBN 0-316-13994-7
10   9   8

MV  NY

*Published simultaneously in Canada*
*by Little, Brown & Company (Canada) Limited*

Printed in the United States of America

*To the McEligots,*
*Lee, John, Jack, Sue,*
*Michael, Mark and Michelle*

*Face-Off*

# 1

WATCH OUT for the falls!"
The yell came from one of the
two boys standing on the bank beside the
frozen pond.

Scott Harrison, skating past a marker
— one of two large rocks placed about
twenty feet apart on the ice — glanced at
the edge of the pond some thirty feet
away, and heard the roar of the falls
in the clear, silent air. He grinned. No
chance!

He turned as sharply as he could
around the marker, noticing that Pete

3

Sewell, the kid he was racing, had just reached his marker. And he had given Pete a twenty-foot handicap, too!

Scott sped down the pond and reached the spot on the ice opposite Cathy, his younger sister, who was refereeing the race.

"The winner!" Cathy yelled, lifting her hands and jumping up on the toes of her skates.

Scott jumped and spun in midair, landing on one skate. He saw Pete cross the invisible line about five feet away and grinned.

"Well," said Pete, skating up to where Scott had stopped beside Cathy, "you did it again."

"You just won't give up, will you, Pete?" Cathy laughed.

Pete's blue eyes twinkled. "One of these days!" he said.

Scott remembered the warning cry from one of the boys on the bank and looked up there. They were sitting on a bench and putting on skates. Even at this distance Scott could see that the skates were the tube kind used in hockey.

"Who are those guys, Scott?" asked Pete.

"I don't know, but they go to our school," said Scott.

"The shorter one is Del Stockton," said Cathy. "I've heard Bev talk about him."

Bev was Judy Kerpa's sister, and Judy was Cathy's friend.

"Who's the tall, skinny kid?" asked Scott.

"I don't know."

Scott dug the toe of his right skate into the ice and skated off toward the center, whipping first to the left and then swinging in a circle around to the right and

5

back again in a beautiful figure eight.

"Hey, Scott! Wait a minute!"

Scott pulled up short and saw the two boys skating toward him. The shorter one, Del Stockton, waved.

They pulled up in front of Scott, ice chips flying as they came to a quick stop. "Hi!" said the shorter of the two. "I'm Del Stockton and this is Skinny McCay. I've seen you at our school."

"I've seen you, too," said Scott, wondering how they knew his name.

"Mind racing with me?"

Scott looked at him in surprise. Del was his height and a few pounds lighter. "Why?"

Del grinned and shrugged. His cheeks were pink from the cold. "Okay. Forget it."

He started to sprint away when Cathy piped up, "Race with him, Scott."

Del must have heard her, for he quickly stopped and headed back toward them, skating backwards. He was fast, Scott saw, as fast skating backwards as some kids were skating frontwards. Scott glared at Cathy, thinking, *You had to open your big mouth.*

"We're not betting money," explained Del. "It's just for fun."

"Go ahead, Scott," urged Cathy. "If there's no bet, what're you afraid of?"

Scott shot another glaring look at her. One thing about Cathy: for a young squirt she wasn't afraid to say what she thought. Nor, sometimes, did she care whom she embarrassed. Like now.

"Aw, Del," Skinny McCay spoke up for the first time. "He's bashful. Let him alone."

"Yeah, okay." Del grinned again. "Forget it, Scott. I shouldn't have asked."

7

He started away again, but hadn't gone more than a yard when Scott stopped him. "Okay. I'll race with you."

"Good!" Del swung around in a half-circle and came to a quick stop in front of Scott. "You pick out the starting point and the finish line."

"Down here," Cathy said, and led the group a short distance down the ice to the spot where Scott had started his race with Pete Sewell. It was between two trees that stood opposite each other on the banks flanking the pond.

"Down around those two rocks and back," said Del. "Okay?"

"Okay," echoed Scott. "Give us the count, Cath."

The boys stood in line and crouched, ready to go.

"One! Two! Three! Go!" yelled Cathy, and the boys took off, their skates biting into the ice as they sprinted toward the

8

rocks about eighty yards away. *Phut! Phut! Phut!* It was a language only ice skates could speak.

They were even most of the way. Then Scott pulled ahead. He stayed ahead as he reached the rock on the right-hand side and skated sharply around it, keeping his turning circle less than five feet beyond the rock. Heading back on the return trip to the finish line he glanced at Del Stockton and saw the boy make the turn even more sharply around the rock on the left-hand side.

Del had gained a few feet on Scott as he came around the turn, but Scott remained in the lead by about four feet. Del stepped up his pace, his arms swinging back and forth as he tried to close the gap between him and Scott.

"Come on, Scott! Come on!" yelled Cathy.

Scott put on more speed. He crossed

the finish line and knew he had won, even if Cathy hadn't jumped and shouted as she did. "You won, Scott! You won!"

He slowed up and glided around to meet Del coming toward him. They stopped and Del stuck out his hand, smiling. "I guess I should have kept my mouth shut," he said. "You're really a fast skater."

"Thanks," said Scott.

"Can you skate backwards?"

"Hardly."

"You ought to practice it," suggested Del.

Scott noticed Del's skates, and also Skinny McCay's. "They're hockey skates, aren't they?" he asked.

"Right," said Del. "Ever play hockey?"

"Never."

"Be at Cass Rink tonight at six-thirty," said Skinny. "We play with the Golden Bears in the Bantam Hockey League. If you want to play, maybe Coach Roberts will put you on one of the lines."

Scott had thought about playing hockey, but had never had the nerve to go out for it.

"You think he would?" he asked, trying not to show how pleased he was at the prospect of playing.

"You're a lot faster skater than most of the guys we've got," said Del. "He should."

"We'll be the Three Icekateers," smiled Skinny.

For a long minute Scott stood there, moving back and forth on his skates. Cathy and Pete were jabbering about something, but he didn't hear a word they said.

# 2

"THERE'S ONE CATCH," said Del. "If you play you'll have to get your own stick and skates. Those won't do." He pointed at the flat-bottomed skates Scott was wearing.

"You can get your stuff at Fred's Sporting Goods," drawled Skinny. "Tell 'em you're playing with us and they'll give you a discount."

Scott thought of the mailbox bank in his room where he put his allowance each week and whatever money he earned from shoveling neighbors' sidewalks and driveways. He figured he must have be-

13

tween eight to twelve dollars, hardly enough to buy a hockey stick and skates.

He looked at his wristwatch and saw that it was close to five-thirty. Mom would have supper ready in fifteen to twenty minutes. Six-thirty would come before he knew it.

"C'mon, Cath," he said, "We'd better get home. So long, Del . . . Skinny! Glad to have met you!"

"Same here!" they called back to him.

Scott and Cathy skated to the bench, took off their skates, and put on their shoes. Pete went along with them. He lived next door. Because he had no brother or sister he usually trailed after either Scott and Cathy or one of the other neighbors.

They walked home, their skates strung over their shoulders. It was a ten-minute walk to Chippewa, the Indian name given to their street. The name of the town was Shattuck. Scott and Cathy had lived here all their lives.

Pete said good-bye and walked up the snow-packed driveway leading to his home. As Scott and Cathy walked up their own driveway they saw a light in the garage and figured that Dad was tinkering with the car again.

"Hi, Dad!" shouted Scott.

"Hello!" came Dad's voice from inside the garage. As the children headed for the kitchen door they saw Dad crouched over the right front fender, his head hidden behind the upraised hood of the car.

"Tell Mother I'll be in for supper in two shakes!" he yelled to them.

Scott smelled something good cooking the moment he opened the door. "Chicken and dumplings!" he cried. "Man! Will I go for that!"

"Was wondering how soon you'd be home," said Mom, coming in from the dining room, where she had just set the table. She looked like a young girl with her dark hair cut in bangs and her figure trim. "Hurry. Supper's about ready."

Both Scott and Cathy were finished washing when Dad came in. He tossed his coat over a chair, then washed his greasy hands. He was all of six feet tall, broad-shouldered and muscular. His stomach bulged a little bit, though, a condition Mom — and sometimes the children — kidded him about.

They sat at the table and said in unison, "Bless this food and us, O Lord, and thank you for the gifts you have given us this day. Amen."

"And please help me get on the Golden Bears hockey team," added Scott.

Three pairs of eyes focused on him. "What was that?" asked Dad.

16

"He's going to play hockey with the Golden Bears!" Cathy cried before Scott had a chance to answer.

"Wait a minute, will you?" snapped Scott. "Nobody is *sure* I am."

"All right," said Mom. "Back off, both of you, and let's hear it from the beginning — from Scott."

Scott sighed. "Well," he began, and told it from the beginning, except that there wasn't much to tell and he had to leave soon to be at Cass Rink by six-thirty.

"So you have to furnish a hockey stick and skates yourself," said Dad.

"I haven't checked my bank yet," said Scott, "but I don't think I've enough to buy both. I'm going to ask Buck Weaver if I can sell papers for him for a week. I know he'll let me. He hates his paper route in the wintertime."

He arrived at Cass Rink a few minutes before six-thirty. It was crowded with

17

kids, and so noisy you couldn't hear yourself think. All except three boys wore regular clothes, with sweaters or jackets. Each had on a helmet and each had a hockey stick and wore skates. The three boys, Scott was sure, were goalies from the looks of their heavy, padded uniforms, extra-large sticks and shin guards.

"There he is!" a voice shouted above the din. "Hey, Scott!"

Skinny McCay broke from the crowd and sprinted toward him. Del trailed. He didn't seem as excited about seeing Scott as Skinny did.

"Hi," greeted Scott. He felt jittery, scared. "Everybody's got a stick," he said. "And a helmet."

"Don't worry," drawled Skinny. "Coach Roberts will get you a stick and a helmet even if he has to take it from somebody."

Scott smiled. If Skinny skated as slowly

as he talked he would be next to useless!

"C'mon," said Skinny. "We'll introduce you to Coach Roberts."

We? Del didn't seem to care whether he went along or not.

Scott saw a man surrounded by several kids near the goal netting and followed Skinny to him.

"Coach Roberts!" cried Skinny.

The coach looked up. He was tall and thin and wore a blue turtleneck sweater. "Hi, Skinny."

Skinny skated up to him with Scott close behind. "This is the kid I was telling you about, Coach. Scott Harrison."

The coach smiled and put out his hand. Scott gripped it. "Hi, Scott. Heard you beat Del Stockton in a race."

Scott shrugged shyly.

"Ever play hockey?"

"Just shinny," said Scott.

"Then you've got some learning to do. But don't worry. It won't take you long — not if you're fast on your skates." He glanced at Scott's skates. "You'll have to get hockey skates. But I'll let you get away with those today. Don't you have a stick?"

"No."

The coach looked at a stocky boy beside him. "Fat, there are a couple on a bench in the locker room. Bring one, will you, please?"

Fat squirted away.

Skinny nudged Scott. "Fat's my brother," he said. "You wouldn't believe it, but he plays center. So do I."

"When you buy your hockey stick, hold it in your hands and test it for its length, weight and lie," said Coach Roberts. "The lie is the angle the blade makes with the shaft. You will also have to get a helmet and a mouth guard. We'll furnish the rest. Okay?"

Scott smiled. "Okay."

Del arrived with the stick and handed it to Scott. It was taped near the bottom of the blade and slightly battered.

Coach Roberts blew a blast on his whistle. "Okay, men!" he shouted. "Gather around me a minute!"

The boys skated toward him like a swarm of bees.

"We've practiced a week already, so nearly all of you boys know what to do," said the coach. "We have a new member starting with us tonight. Scott Harrison. He's a good skater, and if we can mold him into a good puck handler I'm sure he'll help our team very much. Skinny, come here beside me. The rest of you line up next to Skinny, with Del Stockton next to last. Scott, you're tail-end Charlie. You follow Del."

The boys hustled into position.

"Okay, follow me," said the coach.

He skated diagonally down the length of the rink toward the corner, circled gracefully behind the goal close to the boards, then skated diagonally across the length of the rink and behind the other goal. He circled that and retraced his path down the rink again and around the goal, the boys following smoothly behind him and copying his every move. Scott realized that the drill taught them to make turns both ways.

He felt an excitement more joyous than he had ever felt skating whichever way he wished on a pond. There was something special about skating with a bunch of hockey players.

The coach suddenly blew a blast on his whistle. Scott, watching Del closely, saw a gap between him and Del quickly widen. He realized then that the blast meant an increase in speed.

He dug his skates hard into the ice. As

he reached the corner and tried to skate smoothly around the curve — one foot crossing over the other in swift, pistonlike motions — the back of his left skate struck the front of his right and knocked him off-balance.

He spun. His knees wobbled. He reached out for something to grab, but there was nothing, and down he went.

Del looked back at him and laughed. "You just lost your membership, speedy!" he cried.

Scott clambered to his feet. "What?"

"Okay, we'll give you another chance," said Del, skating up beside him. "But one more bad goof and you're no longer an Icekateer. Got it?"

# 3

SCOTT STARED, deeply hurt. Was Del serious? If he was, he's not giving me much of a chance, thought Scott. After all, this is only my first practice. And I have never skated in a drill before.

Skinny eased up beside him when the drill was over. "Don't let Del bother you," he said quietly. "He didn't like the idea of my asking you to be one of us Icekateers. That's why he popped off."

"Maybe I'd better not be," replied Scott. "Not till I can prove to him I'm as good as he is."

Skinny shrugged. "Okay. If that's the way you want it."

"What is the Icekateers, Skinny? A club?"

"No, not really. It's just something special between Del and me. We said that we'd bring in another guy if he was real good, though. That's why I had asked you."

"Hadn't you talked it over first?"

"Well . . . a little." He seemed reluctant to talk about it any further.

"Okay, Skinny," said Scott. "I appreciate your asking me, anyway."

Next came the "skate-the-square" drill. The coach had the boys divide into three teams, placed gloves at eight points on the ice, which, using the face-off spots also as points, formed three squares. Then he had each team skate around a square.

For a while they just skated, the leader

26

of each team starting off at a slow pace and gradually going faster.

After a while the coach gave the lead man a puck. The man skated around the square twice, then passed the puck to the man behind him.

Here's where I flunk, too, thought Scott.

He watched how each man stickhandled the puck, dribbling it along the ice with quick changes of the stick from one side of the puck to the other — zigzagging it. The closer the puck came to him the more nervous he became.

He watched Del stickhandle the puck like an expert. After skating around the square twice Del backpassed the puck to him.

"All yours, Scott!" cried Del.

The pass was a fast wrist-snap. And Del had shot it a fraction of a second before he had yelled, catching Scott off guard.

Scott reached for the puck, but too late. The black pellet zipped past the blade of his stick across the ice toward the boards, and Scott looked at Del.

"That was your second chance, Harrison!" yelled Del. "And you blew it! You know what *that* means!"

Yes, I know! thought Scott. But you wanted me to miss it, you fink! You wanted me to look bad! You hate to see another guy skate as well as you or Skinny!

He sprinted after the puck, intercepted it as it bounced off the boards, then dribbled it up the ice ahead of him. He had done this before while playing shinny, dribbling it back and forth while he skated as fast as he could. He didn't remember ever being nervous before, but he was nervous now. He was tense as a board. Everybody was watching him.

The puck got away from him at the corner.

"Hook your stick around the puck at the sharp turns, Scott!" he heard Coach Roberts advise.

He retrieved the puck, skated straight down to the next corner, then hooked his stick around the puck as he cut sharply at the turn. At the same time he reduced his speed. He made the maneuver without losing the puck and heard the coach say, "That's the way to do it, Scott!"

He completed the circle, went around again, and the coach called the drill to a halt.

"All right. Practice shooting from the blue lines now," he ordered. "Line One on the north goal. Line Two on the south goal. Line Three, rest up till I call you. Scott, stay with Line Two. I want you to work out as a defenseman."

Skinny poked him with his stick and grinned. "You're with us, buddy!" he said.

"Did you see what Del did?" asked Scott.

"I saw him shoot the pass to you," replied Skinny. "Why?"

"He shot before he yelled. He wanted me to miss it on purpose."

Skinny frowned, as if he couldn't believe it.

"I'm not kidding," said Scott. "He did it on purpose. He wanted me to look bad."

"He had no reason to do that," broke in Fat, who had skated up beside him. "I saw that pass. You should've had it."

Scott blushed and suddenly realized that Fat might as well have called him a liar.

"Listen, mister," said Fat, "in this sport you can be a fast skater. But if you're not ready every second you're worthless."

Scott, his face still burning, knew that there was no use saying anything more to either Fat or Skinny. Fat was on Del's side. And Skinny, being an Icekateer, favored Del, too. I might as well keep my mouth shut, thought Scott, otherwise I'll get into hotter water.

He turned and skated along with Skinny to the blue line facing one of the goals, and saw Del Stockton joining them. The other players lining up side by side at the blue line and playing with Line Two were Bernie Fredricks, Joe Zimmer and Vern Mitchell. Paul Carson, a short kid wearing heavy goalie gear, skated to the crease inside the goal. What equipment he had to wear, thought Scott without envy. Leg pads, chest protector, padded jacket, heavy goal gloves. Man! And his stick was really reinforced, too, with white adhesive tape over the heel and partway up the shaft.

The coach gave each line a puck. "Okay.

31

Start with the man on the left. Dribble to within five feet of the goal and shoot. Follow up on the rebounds."

Del led off for Line Two. He sped toward the goal, dribbling the puck with his head and eyes up, looking at the goal but dribbling the puck as if he were looking at it and the goal at the same time. Wow! thought Scott. No matter what kind of a guy Del was, he could really stickhandle!

Del got to within five feet of the goal, shifted his stick quickly to one side of the puck, then the other, then shot. Paul Carson dove toward the corner where the puck headed like a little black rocket, but missed it.

Bernie Fredricks was next. He dribbled the puck toward the goal, shot, and Paul stopped it with his stick. The puck glanced off toward the boards. Bernie skated after it, caught the rebound, bolted around the

back of the goal and shot again. Again Paul stopped it.

"Okay," said the coach. "Next man."

Paul shot the puck across the ice to Joe Zimmer, who dribbled down, fired at the goal, and missed it. He came around with the rebound and fired again. This time the puck flew over Paul's left shoulder and landed against the net behind him.

"Nice shot, Joe!" said the coach.

Skinny dribbled the puck down the ice like a bullet, zigzagged it as he got near the goal, then shot. The puck skittered past Paul's left skate and against the net.

At last it was Scott's turn. Butterflies fluttered around in his stomach as he dribbled the puck down the ice, got close to the goal and fired it toward the narrow space between Paul's left skate and the side of the net. Paul's foot shot out and kicked the puck toward the boards. Scott raced after it, caught the rebound, and sped around the back of the goal. He saw Paul covering the side of the net like a blanket, and skated by, dribbling the puck with all the experience he had gained while playing shinny on the frozen pond near home.

From the corner of his eye he saw the opening between Paul's legs. Snap! He shot the puck directly through them.

"Nice shot, Scott!" yelled the coach.

Scott returned to the blue line, feeling good.

They continued the shooting practice for twenty minutes. Line Three went in to take Line One's place after ten minutes of play, rested ten minutes, then took Line Two's place. In this way each line had a total of twenty minutes of practice shooting.

They were sweating as they skated off

the ice and into the locker room after the drills. Scott was pooped. Some of the boys bought cold drinks from the automatic dispenser. Scott couldn't. He hadn't brought any change with him.

Skinny came over with two opened bottles. "Here. Take one," he said, grinning.

Scott did. "Thanks!"

Del approached with a soft drink and sat next to Skinny. He ignored Scott completely.

# 4

COACH ROBERTS gave Scott an approval form to be filled out by his parents and another form to be completed by his doctor after a physical examination. Mom and Dad signed the approval form, which meant that they were letting him play with the Golden Bears hockey team.

At school the next day he asked Buck Weaver if Buck would like to take a vacation from his paper route next week. Buck was a tall kid with hair like straw and a face showered with freckles.

"In this crummy weather I'd like a two-week vacation," said Buck. "Why?"

37

"I need a pair of hockey skates and a stick," replied Scott. "I'd like it for a week. Starting Monday."

"It's yours," replied Buck. "But I've picked up more customers since the last time you went around with me."

"How many have you got now?"

"One hundred and nineteen. I'll keep a cent on each paper, like before."

"It's a deal," said Scott. They shook hands to clinch it.

Right after school Scott took the doctor's form to Dr. Wilkins' office five blocks away. It was snowing and he trotted most of the way. The doctor examined him thoroughly and passed him with flying colors.

"So you're going to play hockey," said Dr. Wilkins, a thin man with a fine-looking crop of black hair slightly sprinkled with gray. His head had been as bald as an egg the last time Scott had seen him. Boy! thought Scott. What a wig can do to a guy!

"It's rough but a lot of fun," remarked Scott, and went out the door. By the time he reached home snow had collected like a thick blanket on his hat and shoulders. He rubbed it off before going into the house, where he removed his rubbers and placed them on a mat.

"Well," said Mom, "Dr. Wilkins find anything wrong with you?"

"Not a thing," replied Scott, pulling off his coat and hat. "Is Dad home yet?"

"It's only four o'clock," said Mom. "He won't be home for another hour and fifteen minutes. Why?"

"Buck Weaver is letting me take his paper route next week. I won't have all the money I'll need to buy a hockey stick and skates till then." He paused. "I was

39

wondering, could you lend me what I need now? I'll pay you back next weekend."

"Of course," said Mom. "I won't lend you money, though. I'll use my credit card. You can pay me when the bill comes."

Scott grinned. "Fine, Mom! Can we get them now? It shouldn't take long."

"Do you know where to go?"

"Yes. Fred's Sporting Goods Store."

"Okay. Put your rubbers and coat back on and I'll get ready."

Footsteps pounded in from the dining room. "Can I go, too?" asked Cathy.

"Me and my shadow," grunted Scott.

"Come on," said Mom.

In less than five minutes they were in the white Volkswagen, rumbling up the street, the windshield wipers snapping back and forth. In another five minutes

40

they were inside Fred's Sporting Goods Store.

Fred showed Scott half a dozen hockey sticks, each with a different size lie. "The lie is the angle of the blade with the shaft, you know," he told Scott. "Try each one. See which fits you the best."

Scott tried each one. They all fitted pretty well. He picked up the third one again, tested it for balance, weight and lie and decided that this was it.

"I also need hockey skates," he said. "Size eight and a half."

Fred lifted a box off the shelf and took out a sharp-looking pair of shoeskates.

Scott tried them on. He stood on a rug with them. They felt great. "I'll take them," he said.

"You've got a good pair there," said Fred. "Should last you through a lot of games. Whose team are you on?"

41

"The Golden Bears," said Scott.

"Fine. I know your coach. Dick Roberts. Good man. Knows his hockey. Hope you have a good year." He handed the wrapped-up skates and stick to Scott.

"Thanks," said Scott.

He was set now. All he needed was the uniform, and he'd get that from Coach Roberts.

At practice that evening the coach divided the Golden Bears into two teams and had them shinny for fifteen minutes to loosen up their skating muscles. Next was a fifteen-minute period of skating from the blue line toward the goal and then shooting. Then followed a "start and stop" drill during which all the players skated from one end of the rink to the other and back again. Whenever Coach Roberts blew his whistle, the men would come to a quick stop, then start again when the coach gave another blow on the whistle. This drill was supposed to toughen and condition the skating muscles, and develop the sudden stop and start skill.

Scott saw that some of the guys skidded three or four feet before stopping. He didn't. He stopped almost the instant he heard the whistle blow, with both skates turned sharply at an angle, shooting up sprays of ice.

Learning how to bodycheck came next. A lot of the guys knew how already. Scott had seen it done during shinny, but had never really learned the technique.

"Bodychecking is another name for shoulderchecking," explained Coach Roberts. "Keep your body bent forward when you bodycheck or you'll be knocked flat on your back. Keep your legs apart and step into the man you're checking with

43

your shoulder striking his. Make sure your stick is kept down. If it's up you could hurt him. And whether you hurt him or not the ref could send you to the penalty box for high-sticking."

He dropped the puck on the ice. "Del, go after it," he said.

Del did. The coach leaned forward. Just as Del passed the puck with his stick, the coach rammed into Del's left shoulder with his right, knocking Del back.

"That's how it's done," he said. "Except that you'll get hit much harder. Or, if you're doing the bodychecking, you will *hit* much harder. Okay, Scott, go after the puck. Del, bodycheck him."

Scott skated toward the puck as he had seen Del do. He kept shifting his eyes from the puck to Del and back to the puck, wondering just how hard Del would hit him. Just as he reached the puck and struck it, Del bolted into him.

45

The surprise blow from the right shoulder instead of the left, and the hard contact, knocked Scott back. He lost his balance and went down. The guys burst out laughing.

Scott rose to his feet, red-faced. Del grinned.

"Cut the laugh," said the coach. "Scott, he surprised you by hitting you with his right shoulder. That's why you went down. You were also looking down and up from the puck to Del, waiting for him to bodycheck you. Now, listen closely. The time to bodycheck a man is when he least expects it. Just when he passes the puck. Del," he said, tossing the puck some five feet in front of him, "go after it. Bodycheck him, Scott."

Del went after the puck, his stick held out in front of him. Scott shot forward like an uncoiled spring. Just as Del's stick

46

blade touched the puck Scott hit Del's shoulder with his left shoulder, and stopped Del cold.

"Good work, Scott!" cried the coach.

Scott saw Del's surprised look and turned away, a faint smile playing on his face.

"Boys," said the coach, "once you're in uniform I want you to work on bodychecking all you can. It's one of the techniques that helps make a good defensive team. Okay. Let's head for the locker room. Got something for you."

What he had for them were in boxes piled up beside a row of lockers. He tossed a box to each man, whose reaction was a loud, happy yell before tearing open the box and yanking out its contents — a gold uniform with black trim and white numbers.

Scott held his up proudly, then turned

47

it around and looked at the number on the back of the jersey: 12.

"Pretty neat," said a voice beside him. "Think you can earn it?"

Before Scott could answer, Del Stockton walked away.

# 5

SCOTT REMEMBERED every one of Buck Weaver's customers except the new ones Buck had picked up, and Buck had given him addresses for these. The temperature was down around thirty-five on Monday, but the sun was shining.

He made the deliveries on foot and in two trips. The first trip was to the customers at the right of his house, the second at the left. The total delivery time was one hour and fifty-two minutes. He kept track by his wristwatch.

That night was devoted to hard drills: skating frontwards and backwards, shooting at the goal with long and short shots, quick starts and stops, bodychecking and, finally, scrimmaging.

He avoided Del as much as he could. He felt guilty doing so, since it was partly because of Del that he was on the Golden Bears' team.

Being close to Fat McCay bothered him, too. But Fat greeted him with a soft "Hi," and Scott returned the greeting, hoping that no rift would develop between them. He didn't want to risk losing Skinny's friendship over a silly argument with Fat.

Coach Roberts played Scott at right defense, Joe Zimmer at left defense, Bernie Fredricks at right forward, Skinny McCay at left forward, Del Stockton at center on Line Two. Paul Carson was the goalie.

They started the scrimmage against Line One with Coach Roberts acting as referee. Line One's center, Art Fisher, was two inches taller than Del. But when the coach dropped the puck in the face-off Del showed that what he lacked in height he had in speed.

He grabbed the puck with a quick flash of his stick, dribbled it past the red middle line, and snapped it to his left wingman, Skinny McCay. Skinny grabbed it and dribbled it across Line One's blue line. Bill Thomas, Line One's chunky right defenseman, bodychecked Skinny and sent him spinning. He then passed to his center, Art Fisher, who dribbled the puck a bit then passed it across the red line to a teammate skating hard down center ice.

Scott saw the play coming the moment he saw Art looking for a receiver. The teammate was Buggsy Smith, Line One's fast left forward. Buggsy reached for the puck as it sizzled across the ice toward him, but he never got it.

51

Scott had hooked it with his stick. He brought the puck around in front of him, started to dribble it forward, and crash! Someone struck him like a ton of steel. A shower of stars splashed up in front of him like a Fourth of July celebration and he fell. He sat there, waiting for the stars to vanish. In a few seconds they did, and he saw Bill Thomas taking off with the puck.

"Hurry up, Scott!" shouted Coach Roberts. "Cover your position!"

He clambered to his feet and sprinted toward the net. Left defenseman Joe Zimmer was skating hard after Bill, and so were the two wingmen, Del Stockton and Bernie Fredricks.

Bill shuffled the tiny black disk back and forth as he got near the net, then gave it a quick wrist-snap. Goalie Paul Carson, jerking his large stick back and forth in front of the net to match Bill's quick movement, wasn't fast enough to stop it. The puck sailed past him and into the net for a goal.

"H'ray!" shouted the Line One players.

Scott started to circle back to his position at right defense and saw Skinny Mc-Cay swing around in front of him.

"You okay?"

"Yeah."

"All right!" yelled Coach Roberts. "Line Two, out! Come in, Line Three!"

Scott glanced over at Del as the six men of Line Two, including the goalie, skated off the ice. Del's head was down. He seemed deep in thought.

*I know what he's thinking,* thought Scott. *He's wishing that he and Skinny had never asked me to play with the Golden Bears.*

The scrimmage lasted another twenty

minutes. The boys assembled in the locker room, took off their skates and put on their shoes.

"We'll scrimmage every night this week except Friday," announced the coach. "Most of you are pretty green yet. You need a lot of polishing up. See you tomorrow night."

He saw them the next night, the next and the next. On Thursday night he had the team devote the evening to scrimmaging between the lines. Line Two, on the ice with Line Three, got the puck from face-off as Del socked the disk across to his left wingman, Skinny McCay.

"Watch that hanger!" yelled a Line Three man.

Scott looked and saw Bernie Fredricks standing near the red line, a few feet behind and to the left of a Line Two defenseman.

The warning came in time. Skinny shot the puck to Bernie, but a second defenseman had spun about, intercepted the pass, and was dribbling it back down the ice.

Scott sprinted toward him. When he was within six feet in front of the puck carrier, the man brought his stick far back and swung it in a vicious arc at the puck.

Without thinking, Scott covered his face and closed his eyes. He waited for the sound of the stick smacking the puck. Instead, he heard the quick scraping of skates. He dropped his arm and opened his eyes.

Where the defenseman had stood was now an empty space!

Scott glanced toward the goal, just in time to see the man sprinting toward it. Snap! Like a bullet the puck shot past Paul Carson's legs and into the net.

A yell rang out from the members of

Line Three. They jumped and hollered as if this were a real league game.

Suddenly their voices died. Scott saw the guys look at each other, say something, then look at him.

"You freaked out, Scott!" Del yelled at him. "You really freaked out!"

Scott stared at him. "What?"

"What?" echoed Del. "You're puck shy, that's what!"

Scott stood as if frozen.

The league games hadn't even started yet and he was already knee-deep in trouble with Del Stockton. Now something new had sprung to make his playing hockey that much tougher.

He was afraid of the puck.

# 6

THE FACE-OFF.

Fat McCay, center for Line Three, beat Del to the puck and passed it to David Wink, his left wingman. David dribbled the puck across the blue line and then the red line, then passed it to Fat who was skating hard down center ice.

Fat hooked the puck with his stick, shoved it to his left and began to dribble it toward the corner.

"Get it, Scott!"

Scott recognized Del's voice.

"Sure! Get it, Scott!" echoed Fat.

Scott saw the smile on his round, red-cheeked face. Fat was small and chunky, the exact opposite of Skinny. But his skill on the ice was deceptive. He was faster than he looked.

Scott bolted after him, his stick stretched forward to poke check the puck. Just then Fat yelled, "Look out!" and pulled back his stick to belt the puck.

Scott covered his face and closed his eyes. He couldn't help it. He waited for that sound — the sound that would tell him that Fat had smacked the puck.

Instead, laughter exploded close to him, followed by the sound of skates *phut-phutting* by. He saw Fat dribbling the puck toward the goal, no one in front of him except the goal tender, Paul Carson.

Fat zigzagged the puck as he headed for the crease, the square in front of the net, then passed the disk to a man coming from the opposite direction.

Snap! Thud! Just like that the man snapped the puck between Paul's left skate and the corner of the goal and scored.

Again there was a thunderous cry from the men of Line Three. And again Scott saw them looking at him. Looking and smiling as they had done before.

And then he saw Del skate up beside him, his eyes like white rings.

"You did it again, speedy!" he blurted.

Scott blushed.

"When Fat motioned to swing at the puck you covered your face and closed your eyes!" said Del. "Fat saw you do that before when somebody else faked a swing at the puck! So he did it and look what happened! He went by you and you didn't even know it!"

Coach Roberts skated up to them. "What's the trouble?"

"No trouble," said Del, and skated away. Scott headed for his position at right defense.

"Scott," called the coach.

Scott swung around in a quick arc and pulled up in front of Coach Roberts.

"Was he talking about you covering your face when Fat faked a swing at the puck?"

Scott nodded, so ashamed he wished he had never seen a hockey puck.

"Well, don't get sick over it," said the coach. "It happens to some players. You'll just have to condition yourself to stop doing it. Okay. Go to your position."

Scott wasn't able to put himself entirely into the scrimmage after that. He couldn't erase the expression of Del's face from his mind, nor those terrible words: *Puck shy*.

He was glad to get home that night.

The next day he hated to go to school, but he had to. He couldn't tell Mom or Dad why he wanted to stay home. They wouldn't understand.

*Puck shy?* they'd say. *You must be kidding. You mean that you'd stay home because your friends would laugh at you for being a little afraid of the puck? That's ridiculous!*

Grown-ups just don't understand those things.

Time went by quickest during classes. It was the first day that he ever enjoyed classes more than study periods.

That night he rolled and tossed in bed, thinking about the game tomorrow and about Del Stockton. The Golden Bears were playing the Grayhawks, their first game of the season. All he could think of was skating pell-mell toward a puck, then stopping dead cold and covering his face as an opponent pulled back his stick to take a swipe at the little black pellet. And of Del yelling at him. Humiliating him.

What hurt so was that the whole team — all the Golden Bears — knew about his fear, too. How could he play hockey — good hockey — knowing of his weakness?

Somehow he slept. After breakfast he put on his hockey uniform and helmet, got his stick, skates and gloves, and rode with his mother, father and Cathy to Cass Rink.

He kept mum every bit of the way. Once Mom said, "Nervous, Scott? Can't blame you. It's natural. I'm not playing, but I'm probably as nervous as you are."

He didn't say anything.

There was nothing said in the locker room about him. You would think the guys had forgotten all about his puck shyness.

The game started at exactly ten o'clock.

Art Fisher, Line One's center for the Golden Bears, got the puck in the face-off from Jack Young, the Grayhawks' center, and passed it to right wingman Jim Lamont. Jim dribbled it down the ice close to the boards and lost it when a man in a silver uniform with red trim, the Grayhawks' colors, rammed into him in a neat bodycheck. The puck was loose for a few seconds, rolling toward center ice.

A Grayhawk reached it, lifted his stick, swung. The puck rose off the ice and headed like a rocket directly for the Golden Bears' goal. Goalie Cary Small lifted his left gloved hand and caught it.

"Great save, Cary!" yelled the Bears' fans.

Face-off. This time Jack Young won possession of the puck, shot it to a wingman, and sped toward the goal. Golden Bears chased the Grayhawks' wingman

around the back of the net, where he was met by a Golden Bear coming from the opposite direction.

He snapped the puck against the boards. It bounced off, shot toward Jack Young. Cary Small never saw the puck as Jack slapped it past him into the net for a goal.

At the end of four minutes a bell sounded, and Line Two of both teams took over. Scott inhaled deeply as he stepped onto the rink and to his position.

The face-off.

The dropped puck triggered both teams into action. Scott waited tensely, watching the little black disk being struck, poke checked, slapped, and snapped.

Suddenly it shot down the length of the ice. Scott and Joe Zimmer bolted after it. Scott intercepted it behind the net. At the same time the ref's whistle pierced the air and icing was called.

The face-off was between Del and a Grayhawk at the other end of the rink. Sticks clattered. Then Del struck the puck, sent it smack against the boards to his left. It bounced back, directly toward Skinny McCay. At the same time Scott crashed against the boards as a Grayhawk slammed into him. His helmeted head banged against the wall, jarring him.

A whistle stopped the play as the ref waved the offending Grayhawk to "jail" for boarding.

"You want to watch that headhunter, Scott!" yelled Skinny.

Scott smiled. Headhunter was right.

Face-off. Skinny got the puck, dribbled it into Grayhawk territory. He passed to Del. Del caught it, dribbled it toward the goal, shot.

A save!

Del got the puck in the face-off and passed to Skinny. Skinny bolted for the goal, zigzagging the puck with quick movements of his stick, then shot.

The puck sizzled across the ice, banged against the goalie's outstretched skate, and skittered toward the boards.

Scott saw his man charge for the puck and skated after it, too. He flashed by the man and started to reach for the puck. Another Grayhawk popped up from behind the net, stick drawn back to whack the puck.

Scott, only a few feet away from the disk, wanted to go on. He wanted that puck. But a bolt of fear rattled him. The puck had turned into a missile, ready to fly at him.

He covered his face with an arm, and shut his eyes. It was only for a second or

two, but time enough for the Grayhawk
to slap the puck past him.

"Scott!" Del's voice thundered. "Want
a mask?"

# 7

COACH ROBERTS pulled him off the ice and put in Vern Mitchell, the sub.

"Afraid of the puck hitting you, aren't you, Scott?"

Scott's heart was pounding. "I think so."

"The fact is, the puck rises off the ice very seldom," said the coach. "The way it's hit prevents it from rising. Even when a guy pulls back his stick to give the puck a hard whack the chance for it to fly off the ice is slim. Better work on that, Scott. You saw what happened the other night during scrimmage. The boys caught on to your being puck shy. They scared you out of a play and scored. The Grayhawks will do the same thing the minute they catch on."

"They probably did on that play," said Scott softly.

"I wouldn't be surprised."

At the ten-minute time the buzzer sounded again. The two lines went off the ice and Lines Three of both teams went on.

Fat McCay was center for Line Three. The Grayhawks' center was a head taller than Fat, and about twenty pounds lighter. He looked as if he could skate circles around Fat.

But it was Fat who got the puck. Fat who passed it to a wingman. Fat who caught a pass down center ice, dribbled the puck past two defensemen, and then

71

slapped it past the goalie for the first score of the game.

A thunderous shout, mixed with a hard banging of hockey sticks against the boards, sprang from the Golden Bears.

Fat was watched carefully after that. With a minute to go before the three minutes were up Fat tripped a Grayhawk with his stick. Even though he argued with the ref that he had not done it on purpose, he was sent to the penalty box for one minute.

The Grayhawks took advantage of the five-man team and tied the score, 1 to 1.

Line One couldn't break the tie.

Line Two couldn't, either. Scott was so worried that he might do what he had done before that the coach took him out after a minute and a half and put in Vern Mitchell.

"You're worried about it, now, Scott,"

said the coach. "You'll have to settle down."

When the next minute and a half were up, Line Three of both teams got on the ice. This time it was Fat McCay again who scored, putting the Golden Bears ahead, 2 to 1.

The boys sucked on lemons in the locker room during intermission. Coach Roberts perked them up with a short speech, telling them that they "were doing a good job. After all, we're ahead by one goal, and all they got against us is one. So what can I say? Fat, you're doing fine. Just keep it up."

The game resumed. It looked as if the first four minutes would go by scoreless until a surprise slap shot within the last thirty seconds made by the Grayhawks' center, Jack Young, tied the score, 2 to 2.

"Okay, Scott," said the coach as Line

Two went in, "keep your mind on the game. Don't worry about the puck."

The face-off. Burt Stone, centering against Del, got the puck and passed it to a wingman. The wingman dribbled it over the blue line and into Golden Bears territory, flakes of ice spraying from his skates as he sprinted toward the goal.

Joe Zimmer went after him. The Grayhawk skated away from him, and headed directly toward Scott. Scott started to poke-check the puck when the Grayhawk pulled back his stick and started to take a vicious cut at it.

Again the puck turned into a little black monster. And again Scott raised his arm and shut his eyes.

The whistle shrilled, loud and piercing. Scott opened his eyes, dropped his arm, and saw the ref skating toward him, looking and pointing directly at him!

Scott stared.

"High-sticking!" boomed the ref. "The penalty box, fella!"

It was then that Scott realized that this time he had raised his stick-hand to protect his face. He had gone from bad to worse.

# 8

SCOTT HARRISON had to sit in the penalty box for a minute. He was more ashamed than angry. Of all the hockey players he knew only he was shy of the puck. The thing was, he *tried* to keep from lifting his arm. He *tried* to keep from shutting his eyes. But just at the moment when the opponent was going to swing, he'd lose control of himself and seek protection.

"Okay, Scott," said the timekeeper. "Minute's up."

Scott bolted out of the penalty box and onto the ice, determined not to let the puck get the best of him again.

"Let's get on the ball, huh?" said Del, glaring at him.

Del's words, and tone of voice, rattled him. Never had anyone bothered him as much as Del did.

Even Fat's "Come on, Scott! Let's go!" didn't affect him half as much. And it was only because it was Del who, with Skinny, had asked him to join the Golden Bears, thinking that he would be a great help to the team. Instead, he was a burden.

But he wouldn't quit. No one was going to call him a quitter. Even if I never become the good hockey player Del had expected me to be, I'll never quit, he promised himself.

He stayed behind the blue line at the right side of the rink, waiting for the puck to come his way. For thirty seconds Bernie, Skinny, Del and Joe were fighting for

control of the puck against the five Grayhawks. Suddenly Skinny got it and dribbled it hard behind the net. Grayhawks
scampered after him from both sides. Just
as one of them was about to poke check
the puck Skinny banked it against the
boards. Del intercepted it, sped toward
the net, and slammed it. The Grayhawk
goalie fell in front of it for a beautiful
save.

Scott saw Vern Mitchell come onto the
rink and skate hard toward him. *Here I
go*, he thought.

He skated off the ice.

"You're worried about doing the same
thing," said the coach as Scott sat down.
"You'll just have to work on it, buddy. It's
the only way."

The buzzer announced the end of the
three minutes and the lines went off, replaced by Lines Three. Fat almost shot

79

one in after forty seconds of play, but the Grayhawk goalie caught it with his gloved hand.

The Grayhawk center, Jack Young, got control of the puck at face-off and dribbled down center ice. Just as Del swooped upon him to poke-check the puck, the Grayhawk hit it and sent it flying like a rocket through space. It grazed past goalie Steve Hatrack's ear for a goal.

Grayhawk sticks boomed against the boards. They were ahead, 3 to 2.

The Golden Bears fought hard to tie it up, but couldn't. At the end of the game the Grayhawks won, 3 to 2.

In the locker room Scott hurried to get his skates off and his shoes on. He didn't want anyone reminding him of his trouble.

But someone did. Del Stockton.

"I wouldn't believe it if I didn't see it," he said. "You . . . a great skater . . . puck shy!"

"I can't help it," said Scott, his heart pounding.

He got up and started out.

"I just can't believe it," said Del, staring after him.

Scott glared at him. "I heard you!" he cried angrily. "Now leave me alone, will you?" He left the building.

Dad and Mom talked about his problem at home. "Why can't he wear a mask?" suggested Mom.

"Oh, Mom," Scott glowered. "None of the other guys wear masks. Only the goalie. I'll get over it."

Mom looked reflectively at Dad, as if she were wondering whether Scott would or not.

"It's a peculiar reaction," explained Dad. "And I agree with Scott. If he's determined to get over it, he will."

Thanks, Dad, he thought.

He rested after dinner, then telephoned Skinny and asked him if he'd like to play shinny at the ice pond.

"Sure, said Skinny. "I'll bring some guys with me. Okay?"

"Okay," said Scott.

He walked to the frozen pond above the falls, taking along his hockey stick and a puck. Cathy went along. They had walked half a block when a shout came from behind them. Pete Sewell came running up, carrying his skates over his shoulder.

"Hi!" he greeted. "I saw your game this morning, Scott. You played pretty well."

"Right," said Scott. "Just pretty well."

Skinny, Fat, Steve and three other guys

showed up at the pond, and they chose up sides for a game of shinny. Skinny and Fat did the choosing. *Watch,* thought Scott, *I'll be the last one chosen.*

They used a hockey stick to determine who would choose first. Fat tossed it to Skinny. Skinny caught it near the middle. Fat wrapped a hand around it above Skinny's. Then each put his hand above the other's until the top of the hockey stick was reached. The person whose hand covered the stick's end chose first. Skinny won.

Without looking to see who was around him, Skinny said, "Scott Harrison."

Scott couldn't believe it.

Fat chose Steve Hatrack. Finally all the players were chosen. Fat had first choice for the goal and took the one on the falls side. Goals were made simply from small rocks set about five feet apart, one placed

83

some forty feet from the edge of the falls, the other placed where the river narrowed like the shape of a bottleneck. This provided a playing area about sixty feet long.

There was no boy nearby to act as referee, so Cathy volunteered. The boys looked at her suspiciously for a while, and Scott smiled.

"Don't worry about her," he said. "All she has to do is drop the puck in a face-off."

The teams got into position. Skinny and Fat were centers for their teams. Cathy dropped the puck. The centers' sticks clashed with it, and the game was on.

Fat's stick jabbed the puck and sent it skittering across the ice toward the side. Steve bolted after it, hooked it with his stick and dribbled it toward his goal — the goal that was next to the falls. Scott skated after him, came up from behind, and Steve passed to another team member. Scott then sped after him, determined to steal that puck.

Just as he started to reach for it a second opponent came in from his right side and gave him a bodycheck that knocked him off balance. He went down, skidded, got up quickly, and again went after the puck.

A teammate skated up from his defensive position and forced the opponent to turn sharply to his right. As he did so, he saw Scott coming at him. Quickly he raised his stick and brought it down to strike the puck.

Scott shut his eyes, started to lift his arm. And then remembered. *No!* he thought. *I won't get hit by the puck! I won't!*

In that fraction of a second the man struck the puck. It flashed past Scott like a bullet. Scott turned and sprinted after it.

On a rink the play would be icing, for the puck was heading to the left of the goal. The goalie was chasing after it, but he was like a turtle after a rabbit.

Scott skated as fast, or faster, than he had ever skated before. He knew that the falls were just over that curved edge, but the puck was slowing up. He felt sure he could get to it before it reached the edge.

He soon realized that he couldn't, and a wave of horror swept over him. He saw the puck disappear over the edge of the frozen falls. He lowered his body and tried to turn around in a circle to clear the dangerous edge.

He didn't make it. The edge of his skates got too much of a bite in the ice, and he was thrown off balance.

A loud, ear-piercing yell split the air as he left the ice and went hurling through space.

# 9

THE YELL stopped when he saw the swirling white foam rush up at him. He struck the roaring, gushing foam head first. Even as he went under and felt the cold water swallow him he kept his eyes open.

He went down . . . down . . .

Then he began to stroke and kick hard to get to the surface. His clothes and skates were heavy on him. They, and the falls striking the water above him, kept him from rising to the surface. He thought that he would never see daylight again.

His lungs ached for air. He wanted so

much to take a breath, but he knew that doing so would only fill his lungs with water and he might drown.

He looked up and saw water gushing down through the frothy surface, and thousands of air bubbles rising and popping above him. He would never make it to the surface here. The plunging falls would just force him back down.

He swam past the falling water and the bubbles. And, just when he felt his lungs were ready to burst, he broke out of the water, sucked in the cold, fresh air. Although he was wet and freezing, he was so happy he wanted to shout. And he did.

Then he swam to shore, his body feeling as though it weighed a ton. He crawled on his knees to the jagged ice that lined the shore, then got up and walked onto the hard-crusted snow.

Skinny and Fat were the first to reach

him. Behind them came Cathy, her face white as the snow.

"Come on," said Skinny, grabbing his arm, "we've got to get you home."

Fat grabbed his other arm. "You do that for kicks?" he asked.

Scott thought his face would crack as he forced a smile. "Just thought I'd go sw-swimming for a change," he said.

Cathy's watery eyes looked at him. "You — you okay, Scott?"

"I'm f-fine," he stammered.

"Skinny, you're the fastest here," said Fat. "Get his shoes."

While Skinny ran after Scott's shoes, Scott sat on a log and Fat and Cathy took off his skates. Skinny arrived with the dry shoes and the boys put them on.

Scott shivered as he got to his feet and started to run, Cathy beside him. "Better call a doctor the minute you get home," advised Skinny.

Scott arrived home and thought Mom would faint when she saw him in clothes that were caking over with ice.

"Scott!" she screamed. "What happened to you? Get into the bathroom! Take off those clothes and get into the tub as quick as you can!"

"He fell over the falls," explained Cathy.

"Over the *what?*" cried Mom.

"The falls," said Cathy.

Scott got out of his ice-caked clothes and into the tub. He sat shivering in it while he turned on the faucets and waited for the tub to fill. He was still in it, and beginning to feel warm and comfortable, when there was a knock on the door.

"Scott, Dr. Wilkins is here," said his mother's voice.

He climbed out of the tub and, with the towel wrapped around him, he opened the door. Dr. Wilkins smiled at him.

"Well, hello, Scott. You get thawed out?"

Scott grinned. "I think so," he said.

"Let me give you a bodycheck, anyway," said the doctor. "This one won't hurt. Put on your shorts and lie on your bed."

Ten minutes later Dr. Wilkins was taking a small glass container out of his black case and putting it on the nightstand beside Scott's bed.

"Give him two now, then one every four hours until they're all gone," he said to Mrs. Harrison. "And keep him in for the next couple of days."

Scott stared at him. "But Dr. Wilkins, I feel okay!"

The doctor smiled. "This stethoscope tells me different. Don't worry. By Tuesday you'll be good as new."

Tuesday was a long time coming.

# 10

SCOTT PRACTICED with the Golden Bears at Cass Rink on Tuesday, and realized that recuperating for two days had taken some of the strength out of him.

He felt stronger on Wednesday, with one thing on his mind above everything else: *I must stop being afraid of the puck. That's the only way that I can get Del and the rest of the Golden Bears feeling that I'm really one of them.*

The team had intrasquad scrimmage, the lines taking turns playing against each other. The moment that Line Two went in against Line One Scott felt the excitement bubble inside him.

He watched the puck drop from Coach Dick Roberts' hand in the face-off, watched Del Stockton knock it across center ice toward the opposite goal only to be intercepted by Buggsy Smith.

Buggsy dribbled it back across the center line and then socked it hard as Bernie Fredricks scooted at him from the side, his stick stretched out for the puck. Bernie hit Buggsy and both crashed against the boards.

The puck skittered down the ice toward the goal, Scott Harrison and Joe Zimmer bolting after it together. Scott reached it first and belted it back up the ice. An instant later he saw Del Stockton cross in front of him, glaring hotly.

"How about passing it once in a while?" yelled Del.

Scott flushed. In his anxiety to strike the puck up the other end of the rink he had forgotten to look for a receiver.

"The puck, Scott!" someone yelled.

Scott ducked and saw the puck skitter-tering toward him. He hooked it with his stick and dribbled it across the blue and then the center lines. An opponent rushed at him from his right. He put on more speed and stickhandled the puck expertly down the left side of the ice while at the same time he looked for a teammate to pass to.

Del was covered. So were Skinny and Bernie. One man stood in front of the goal, protecting it with the goalie.

For a moment he thought, Should I head for the goal and try a shot? Why not?

He bolted forward. Left defenseman Al Podeski charged at him and tried to slap the puck. Scott stickhandled it away. He faked a shot to Del, who stared as if to say, *Don't pass now, you nut!*

Then Scott skated past the crease in front of the defenseman guarding it. Without slowing up he turned to his right and at the same time snapped the puck past the defenseman's legs, and the goalie's, into the net.

"Well! You did it, man!" yelled Del.

Scott grinned shyly as he skated back down the ice to his position, realizing he had done something probably few of his teammates had noticed. He had scored while skating backwards, a feat he had learned only within the last two weeks.

Coach Roberts blew his whistle and called in Line Three to play against Line Two. "Fine skating, Scott," he said. "Rest awhile; I want Vern Mitchell to get in some practice, too."

The following two nights put him in good shape for Saturday's game against the Beetles. Their name, *Beetles,* and a drawing of a beetle were in bright red on the front of their black satin jerseys.

After a minute and eleven seconds of play Art Fisher knocked in a goal. Thirty seconds later Buggsy rapped one in between the goalie's legs to put the Golden Bears in front, 2 to 0.

Fourteen seconds before the three-minute time was up the red light went on behind the Golden Bears' net for a Beetle score: 2 to 1.

The buzzer sounded. Lines One left the ice and Lines Two came on. The face-off. The scramble for the puck. Scott saw it skitter on its edge toward his side of the rink and sprinted after it. He didn't see the Beetle going after it until both of them were within five or six feet of the puck.

He stretched out his stick. At the same

time the Beetle pulled back his and swung at the puck. For a very brief instant Scott sensed what could happen and lifted his arm. *You're doing it again!*

He dropped his arm. By then the Beetle's stick had swung and struck the disk, sending it like a black bullet down the ice.

"Chicken!" yelled Del as he zoomed by Scott.

Just then a Beetle brushed by him, striking his stick. The impact knocked his stick against another kid's leg. Del's!

Del swerved and came at him, his eyes blazing. He pulled up in front of Scott, his face only inches away, so close Scott felt his warm breath.

"I'm sorry," said Scott. "It was an accident."

"Accident! Yeah!"

"Come on, you guys!" yelled Skinny. "Let's play hockey!"

They broke apart, and Scott saw that

goalie Paul Carson had stopped the puck with his stick and was tossing it to the referee. The ref skated toward the circle to the left and in front of the goal, and waved Skinny McCay and a Beetle to come forward.

The face-off. The battle for the puck. Skinny batted it against the boards and it ricocheted back onto the rink toward the center line. Del scooted after it, dribbled it across his blue line, and passed to Bernie. Bernie nabbed the pass and shot.

A save!

Face-off again. The puck skittered toward center ice. A Beetle belted it. Swish! Down the length of the rink went the puck!

Scott got it behind the net. The whistle shrilled and the ref took the puck to the opposite end of the rink for the face-off.

A Beetle pass! A teammate intercepted

it, dribbled down the ice, then shot. The puck blazed past Scott's legs. He stuck out his stick, but too late. The puck whisked between Paul Carson's outstretched foot and the goal post for the Beetles' second score.

Scott looked at the face that suddenly came into his view.

Say it! he thought. Tell me I should've stopped that shot!

But Del didn't say a word.

# 11

FACE-OFF.

Del Stockton's lightning moves got the puck away from Stinky Marsh, the Beetles' center. Del dribbled it across the Beetles' blue line and was met head-on by two Beetles.

He shot the puck to Skinny McCay skating up from his left side a second before the Beetles crashed into him. Down went all three of them.

Skinny sprinted for the goal, ice spraying from his skates as he stickhandled the puck. Scott, hovering behind the center line, saw a Beetle swooping toward

Skinny, leaving the area behind him wide open. Realizing that this was a good chance to get the puck and try for a goal, Scott bolted forward.

"Skinny!" he shouted.

Skinny snapped the puck. It skittered across the ice toward Scott, who was already skating toward the goal. He stopped the puck with the blade of his stick, took a couple of long, hard strokes, and snap! The Beetle goaltender almost did a split as he kicked his left foot out to stop the streaking puck.

He missed. Goal!

"Nice play, Scott!" cried Skinny, smiling.

"Thanks for the assist," Scott grinned.

Golden Bears 3, Beetles 2.

The face-off. This time Stinky Marsh's fast moves got the puck away from Del. He passed to a teammate, who started to dribble the puck up the center of the ice.

Scott charged after him. The Beetle smacked the puck, sending it whizzing past Scott. Scott sprinted after it, stretching out as far as he could reach with the blade of his stick.

Crash! Down went a player as he tripped over the stick. A Golden Bear!

Oh, no! groaned Scott. It was Del again!

Del went skidding across the ice against the boards. He sat there, glaring at Scott, who skated to him.

"Sorry, Del," Scott apologized, holding out a hand. "I didn't see you."

"Get outa here," muttered Del as he scrambled to his feet.

A second later there was a loud roar, followed by the banging of sticks against the boards, from the Beetles' side. They had scored a goal to tie up the score, 3 to 3.

"They can thank *you* for that," grunted Del.

Scott's heart ached. Del was right. But this time Del should've seen my stick, he told himself. He just couldn't brake in time so he puts the entire blame on me.

Seconds after the face-off the buzzer rang. Lines Two skated off and Lines Three skated on.

"You two are getting pretty reckless out there," observed Coach Roberts bluntly. "What's the matter with you guys?"

"Nothing," said Del.

"I can smell that lie a mile off," replied the coach.

Del's face colored. "He tripped me."

"Tripped you? Why would he want to trip you?"

"I've been yelling at him."

105

"Oh. Why?"

Del shrugged. "He's been making mistakes."

"So? Haven't I been trying to correct them? Or do you think you can do a better job by yelling at him?"

Del looked straight ahead, his ears beet-red. "No, I don't," he admitted. "I'm sorry."

"And I'm surprised," said the coach. "Didn't you and Skinny bring Scott into the club?"

Del nodded.

"I don't know," sighed the coach. "Maybe you're not pleased with Scott's performance. But this is his first season. You've got to give him a chance. Okay. Let's drop the matter right now. One of the easiest ways of losing a hockey match is to have at least two members of the same team cross sticks with each other.

Let's end that of this minute. Okay?" He paused. "Del?"

"Yes, sir."

"Scott?"

"Yes, sir."

"Fine."

They watched the remaining minutes of the game between Lines Three in silence. Lines One took over, and the Beetles knocked in another goal, putting them in front, 4 to 3.

"Let's get 'em back," said Skinny as the buzzer sounded and Lines Two replaced Lines One on the ice.

Face-off. The puck dropped. Sticks clashed. Skates blazed across the ice. Here and there black satin uniforms mixed with the gold. Suddenly, a crash at the side boards. The *Phreeeeep!* of the whistle. Scott saw a Beetle down on the ice, Del Stockton on top of him.

A fight? No. Boarding. One minute in the penalty box. Del rose and skated off, his head drooped.

It was five men against six now. The face-off. The fight for the puck. It skittered toward the boards. Scott, Bernie, Skinny and two Beetles sprinted after it.

Scott, faster than the rest, reached it first. He hooked it with the blade of his stick, spun around, and dribbled across the center line, then the blue. He looked up, saw the Beetle goaltender crouched in front of the goal, legs apart, stick held ready. On each side of him was space.

Scott fired. The puck sailed like a rocket toward the right of the goalie. The goalie's hand snapped at it like the tongue of a frog snapping at a fly. He missed.

Goal!

Thunder resounded as Golden Bear sticks banged against the boards. "That-away to go, Scott!"

Golden Bears 4, Beetles 4.

Again the face-off. Again the struggle for the puck. Then the minute was up. Del came back on the ice. The Bears skated brilliantly. They bodychecked, passed, shot, and shot again. The buzzer sounded. It was time for Lines Three.

Three minutes later the first period was over. The score was still 4 to 4.

"Nice shooting, Scott," said Skinny as they headed for the locker room.

Scott smiled, and looked for Del. Their eyes met for a moment, then Del looked away.

They quenched their thirst with soft drinks and sucked on slices of oranges while Coach Roberts looked proudly at them.

"You guys are playing good hockey," he said. "You're skating fine. A little shy about taking shots, but that's okay. Pass a little more. And pass in *front* of your man, not at him. Watch yourselves about boarding as Del did. Boarding, charging, or illegal bodychecking are violations."

The second period started.

Lines One got on and off without scoring. The Beetles' Line Two threatened in the first thirty seconds when Stinky Marsh belted the puck against goalie Paul Carson's skate from just beyond the crease. The puck ricocheted toward the boards, only to be picked up by Stinky again.

Skating brilliantly he dribbled behind the goal. Scott, suspecting what Stinky was going to do, skated in front of the crease to help Paul defend the goal. Stinky swooped around the corner of the net, brought his stick back, and let it fly at the puck.

Scott saw it leave the ice like a rocket and head for him. He lifted his arm, closed his eyes and ducked.

Crack!

# 12

THE PUCK STRUCK his helmet and glanced over the net against the boards.

Scott stood frozen, his heart pounding. The thought of what had happened hit him, and he sucked in his breath and held it. Around him black and gold uniforms were flashing every which way. A Beetle bumped him. He spun, fell.

A gold uniform appeared before him. He looked up into Skinny McCay's face. "Scott! You okay?"

He nodded, and tried to rise to his feet. His knees were rubbery and he fell again.

*Phreeeeep!* The whistle brought the blur of gold and black uniforms to a stop. The ref skated forward, helped him to his feet, and guided him off the rink. Coach Roberts met him at the gate.

"Scott, you hurt?"

"No."

He was dizzy. He wanted to sit down. The coach helped him to the bench. "Take it easy," he said. "You'll be all right."

He sat down. In a while his head cleared. He saw that Vern Mitchell was in his place, and felt ashamed. He was breathing easier now, but his heart was still pounding and sweat was dribbling down his cheeks into the corners of his mouth.

The coach unsnapped his helmet, took it off, wiped the sweat off with a handker-chief.

"Just relax and watch the rest of the

113

game from the bench," he advised. "You played a good game. You showed a lot of spunk."

"I showed that I'm still scared of the puck," murmured Scott.

"That's all right. You'll get over it. But it takes more than one game, or two games, or even three. It's not easy."

"I'll never get over it," said Scott.

"That's crazy talk, kid. You think you're the only one who's ever had that problem? Some pros have it, too. Yes, pros. I know. I've seen them."

Stinky Marsh scored a half a minute before the three-minute time was up. Fat McCay tied it up when Lines Three went in, but it was Stinky again who later broke the tie. And that was the way the game ended. Beetles 6, Golden Bears 5.

Coach Roberts met Dad and Mom at the exit door.

"Hi, Dick," said Dad. "How's Scott? Think we should keep him off the rink for a while?"

Scott's heart jumped to his throat. He looked from his father to Coach Roberts.

"No. I don't think we ought to get him away from the game entirely. I'll just watch him. Leave him to me."

The coach met Scott's eyes and he winked.

"There's practice Monday at six-thirty," he said. "Can you be there?"

Scott smiled. "Yes."

# 13

SCOTT and Cathy went to the pond Sunday after church and skated till noon. Scott saw that Cathy was keeping a safe distance away from the falls and smiled to himself. He knew she was doing it so that he wouldn't go near them himself.

*Don't worry,* he thought. *Once over those icy falls is enough!*

That afternoon they rode with Dad and Mom in the country. The roads were clear and the snow-covered trees stood erect and still in the white fields. They passed snowmobiles that glided swiftly over the fields, leaving twin trails behind them.

Passing by a mountainside they watched skiers riding on a ski lift to the top of the mountain and skiing down the long, slanting slope. Halfway down, one of the skiers fell, lost a ski, and skidded nearly to the bottom of the hill before he got back on his feet.

It was nearly dark when they returned home. Mom and Cathy put supper on the table and Mom cooked hot chocolate and they ate and talked about the things they had seen.

Scott went to Cass Rink on Monday evening. The Golden Bears practiced skating backwards for fifteen minutes, then worked on bodychecking and hip-checking (bumping the side of the puck-carrier with your hip to knock him off stride), passing and shooting. The last half hour was devoted entirely to scrimmage.

117

The following evenings their practice routine remained the same. By game time Saturday Scott thought he had really licked his problem.

The Golden Bears played the Bullets. When Lines Two took over the ice from Lines One in the first period the score was 1 to 0 in the Bullets' favor.

The Bullets wore gray, red-trimmed uniforms with white letters and numbers. A picture of a bullet with wings on it was on the front of their jerseys. Slim Jason was their center.

The face-off. The dropped puck. The two hockey sticks batting at it. Then Slim struck it solidly, sending it across the Golden Bears' blue line.

Joe Zimmer intercepted it and dribbled it back up the ice. A Bullet rushed at him and Joe passed to Scott. Scott stickhandled the puck across the red line into Bullet territory, saw a Bullet sprinting toward him, and passed to Del. Del shot, missing the goal by a foot.

A Bullet retrieved the puck behind the goal and dribbled up the ice.

"Get back!" Del yelled at Scott.

Scott spun, saw that all five Bears, including himself, had left their side of the rink wide open. He started to skate backwards, his eyes on the puck-carrier. But the Bullet had picked up speed and was sprinting down the side. Scott turned and sped after him. He reached out to hook the puck. The blade of his stick caught the Bullet by the ankle, and down he went.

*Phreeeeep!* went the whistle.

"Nice going!" Del grunted as he skated by.

The ref motioned Scott toward the penalty box, then skated there himself. "Tripping," he said to the timekeeper.

The Bears tried hard to keep the puck down in Bullet territory, but, with twenty seconds remaining of Scott's penalty, Slim Jason blasted a shot past goalie Paul Carson into the net.

The Bullets had the puck in their possession when the timekeeper turned to Scott. "Okay. Time's up."

Scott rushed out onto the ice, eager to make up for that lost minute.

He seemed to have surprised the puck-carrier, for the man glanced around at him wide-eyed as Scott sneaked up from behind him, bodychecked him aside, and stole the puck.

He dribbled the disk across the center line and the blue line with Bullets on both sides of him. He saw Skinny come into his view at his left and passed the puck to him. The pass was good. Skinny caught it with the blade of his stick, dribbled to-

120

ward the Bullets' goal, and wrist-snapped it.

Goal!

Golden Bears' sticks clattered against the boards. "Nice shot, Skinny!" yelled the fans.

Del skated up beside Scott and smiled. "Nice play."

"Thanks," said Scott, who thought, *That's the first nice thing he's said to me in ages.*

The buzzer sounded and the lines skated off, giving the ice over to Lines Three. The Bullets' line proved stronger than the Bears' and scored twice before Fat McCay got hot and banged in two to tie it up again, 3 to 3.

Buggsy assisted with a score and shot one in himself to put the Bears back in the lead, 5 to 3.

Lines Two went back on the ice.

Hardly six seconds ticked off after the drop of the puck when Slim Jason smashed a line drive directly for the goal. The puck shot like a small black meteor at Scott, who was in its way. For the first time in a long time the little black puck turned into a little black monster.

It was shooting directly for his face.

# 14

SCOTT DUCKED.

At the same time he knew that if the puck sailed by him it might shoot past Paul Carson for a goal.

He raised his hand. *Smack!*

The puck struck the pocket of his glove, clung there for just a fraction of a second, then dropped.

"Nice stop, Scott!" yelled Del.

Golden Bears' sticks clattered against the sideboards, and just for a second Scott Harrison smiled. He felt good.

A Bullet sped toward him, hockey stick held out to grab the puck. Like a shot Scott dropped his stick and flicked the puck to Del, whom he saw skating up at his left.

Del caught the pass and dribbled it across the center and then the blue line into Bullet territory. Two Bullet defensemen went after him. Del passed to Skinny and Skinny shot. The puck blazed through the air like a rocket, but the Bullets' goalie stuck out his gloved hand and stopped it.

This time Bullet hockey sticks rattled the sideboards, and cheers rang out for their goalie. "Nice save, Ed!"

Skinny and a Bullet defenseman stood ready for the face-off in the circle at the front left of the Bullets' goal. The puck dropped and Skinny got control of it almost instantly.

He sprinted toward the goal. A guard struck him with a bodycheck, knocked him to the ice, and the puck skittered toward the goal crease. Another guard hooked it with the blade of his stick and whisked it away up the center of the ice.

Scott back-skated hurriedly to cover his zone. Del went after the puck-carrier, who passed to a teammate skating near the sideboards several feet in front of Scott. Scott stopped back-skating and shot forward. Just as he started to reach for the puck the Bullet pulled back his stick and swung.

Scott clamped his eyes shut and raised a hand.

*No! No!* Quickly he opened his eyes and dropped his hand, in time to see the puck whizz past his legs.

The buzzer sounded, ending the three minutes. Lines Two went off, Lines Three went on.

Scott expected Del to remind him of what he'd done, but Del didn't. Nor did Coach Roberts.

Neither team of Lines Three scored and the buzzer sounded, ending the first period.

While Scott sucked on a slice of orange Skinny, sitting beside him, said softly, "Scott, Del ever tell you who really wanted you to play with us?"

Scott frowned. "Wasn't it you?"

"No. It was Del. He'd seen you skate and thought you were the best he'd ever seen."

"You're kidding."

"Ask him," said Skinny.

Scott stared at Skinny a long minute. "I guess I've really disappointed him," he said. "No wonder he acted like he did."

Someone tapped him on the shoulder. He turned and saw that it was Del. Del smiled as he tossed a sucked-out slice of orange into a rubbish can and wiped his mouth. "Not anymore," he said, smiling.

"You sure?"

Del's smile spread. "Look, I think I've learned to keep my mouth shut when I'm supposed to. Oh, by the way, Skinny and I decided we want you with us again."

"As an Icekateer?"

"Of course!"

"Come on, boys!" interrupted Coach Roberts. "On the ice. Hustle!"

Lines One created a lot of action on the rink, but that was all. Lines Two continued the action, with one difference: Slim Jason scored to put the Bullets one point behind the Golden Bears, 5 to 4.

Fat McCay fouled twice for Line Three, keeping him out most of the three minutes and giving the Bullets an opportunity to score twice, going ahead of the Bears, 6 to 5.

"Our last time around," Scott said to Del as Lines One shot the puck all over the rink for three minutes without getting a good shot at the net. The buzzer sounded and Lines Two took over.

"And this is our last chance," said Del. "How do you feel, Scott?"

"Fine."

"Good. Let's knock in a few."

The face-off. The dropped puck. The fight for it. The clatter of sticks. And then Slim Jason had the puck, dribbling it down center ice, ice chips flying from his skates as he sped. He was stickhandling the puck with one hand, zigzagging the disk with speed and the greatest of ease.

Skinny tried to steal the puck away from Slim's right side, Del tried to poke check it from his left. Both Bears were good hockey players, but Slim was better. He was fast, graceful, confident.

And then Scott, covering his zone close to the front and right side of the rink, saw it coming. Slim's stick was rising. He was going to shoot.

Just as his stick hit the puck Scott sprinted in front of the goal, directly in line of its path.

Fear gripped him as he saw it coming at him. But he didn't panic. He didn't shut his eyes. He didn't duck.

Instead, he lifted his hand, stopped the puck, dropped it, then sent it spinning across the ice toward Del. Hockey sticks thundered against the sideboards on the Golden Bears' side.

"Beautiful stop, Scott!"

Scott skated up the ice after the puck. There was a scramble for it, then several shots for the goal. None went in. Moments later the buzzer sounded, and the lines left the ice, replaced by Lines Three.

There was little said on the bench as Lines Three battled for three minutes without scoring. The game ended in the Bullets' favor, 6 to 5.

"No disgrace to lose," said Coach Roberts in the locker room. "You all played an excellent game. Forget this one. There's a new game next week."

"Think you're over being puck shy?" Skinny asked Scott.

"I got a little scared that last time," admitted Scott.

Del looked at him, smiled. "It takes a lot of guts to admit that," he said.

Scott shrugged and put on his shoes. He swung his shoeskates over his shoulder, stood up, and started for the door.

A shout from Del exploded behind him. "Hey, wait for us! We're the Three Icekateers! Remember?"

He smiled as Del and Skinny came up beside him, and together they walked out of the building.

131

# How many of these Matt Christopher sports classics have you read?

## Baseball

❑ Baseball Pals
❑ Catcher with a Glass Arm
❑ Challenge at Second Base
❑ The Diamond Champs
❑ The Fox Steals Home
❑ Hard Drive to Short
❑ The Kid Who Only
   Hit Homers
❑ Little Lefty
❑ Long Stretch at First Base
❑ Look Who's Playing
   First Base
❑ Miracle at the Plate
❑ No Arm in Left Field
❑ Shortstop from Tokyo
❑ The Submarine Pitch
❑ Too Hot to Handle
❑ The Year Mom Won
   the Pennant

## Basketball

❑ The Basket Counts
❑ Johnny Long Legs
❑ Long Shot for Paul
❑ Red-Hot Hightops

## Dirt Bike Racing

❑ Dirt Bike Racer
❑ Dirt Bike Runaway

## Football

❑ Catch That Pass!
❑ The Counterfeit Tackle
❑ Football Fugitive
❑ The Great Quarterback
   Switch
❑ Tight End
❑ Touchdown for Tommy
❑ Tough to Tackle

## Ice Hockey

❑ Face-Off
❑ The Hockey Machine
❑ Ice Magic

## Soccer

❑ Soccer Halfback

## Track

❑ Run, Billy, Run

All available in paperback from Little, Brown and Company

# Join the Matt Christopher Fan Club!

To become an official member of the Matt Christopher Fan Club,
send a self-addressed, stamped envelope (10 x 13, 3 oz. of postage) to:

Matt Christopher Fan Club
34 Beacon Street
Boston, MA 02108